P9-CQG-703

TEN BIRDS

For my mom

Kids Can Press acknowledges the financial support of the Government of Ontario, through the Ontario Media Development Corporation's Ontario Book Initiative; the Ontario Arts Council; the Canada Council for the Arts; and the Government of Canada, through the BPIDP, for our publishing activity.

Published in Canada by
Kids Can Press Ltd.
25 Dockside Drive
Toronto, ON M5A 0B5

Published in the U.S. by
Kids Can Press Ltd.
2250 Military Road
Tonawanda, NY 14150

www.kidscanpress.com

The artwork in this book was rendered in pen and ink on paper.
The text is set in Incognito.

Edited by Tara Walker
Designed by Karen Powers

This book is smyth sewn casebound.
Manufactured in Tseung Kwan O, NT Hong Kong, China, in 10/2010 by Paramount Printing Co. Ltd.

CM 11 0 9 8 7 6 5 4 3 2 1

Library and Archives Canada Cataloguing in Publication

Young, Cybèle, 1972-
Ten birds / Cybèle Young.

ISBN 978-1-55453-568-2

I. Title.

PS8647.O622T46 2011 jC813'.6 C2010-905462-8

Kids Can Press is a Corus™ Entertainment company

TEN BIRDS

Cybèle Young

KIDS CAN PRESS

TEN birds were trying to figure out
how to get to the other side of the river.

The one they called "Brilliant" knew how to cross.
Marching, he left NINE behind.

The one they called "Quite Advanced" engineered her way.
Bubbling, she left EIGHT behind.

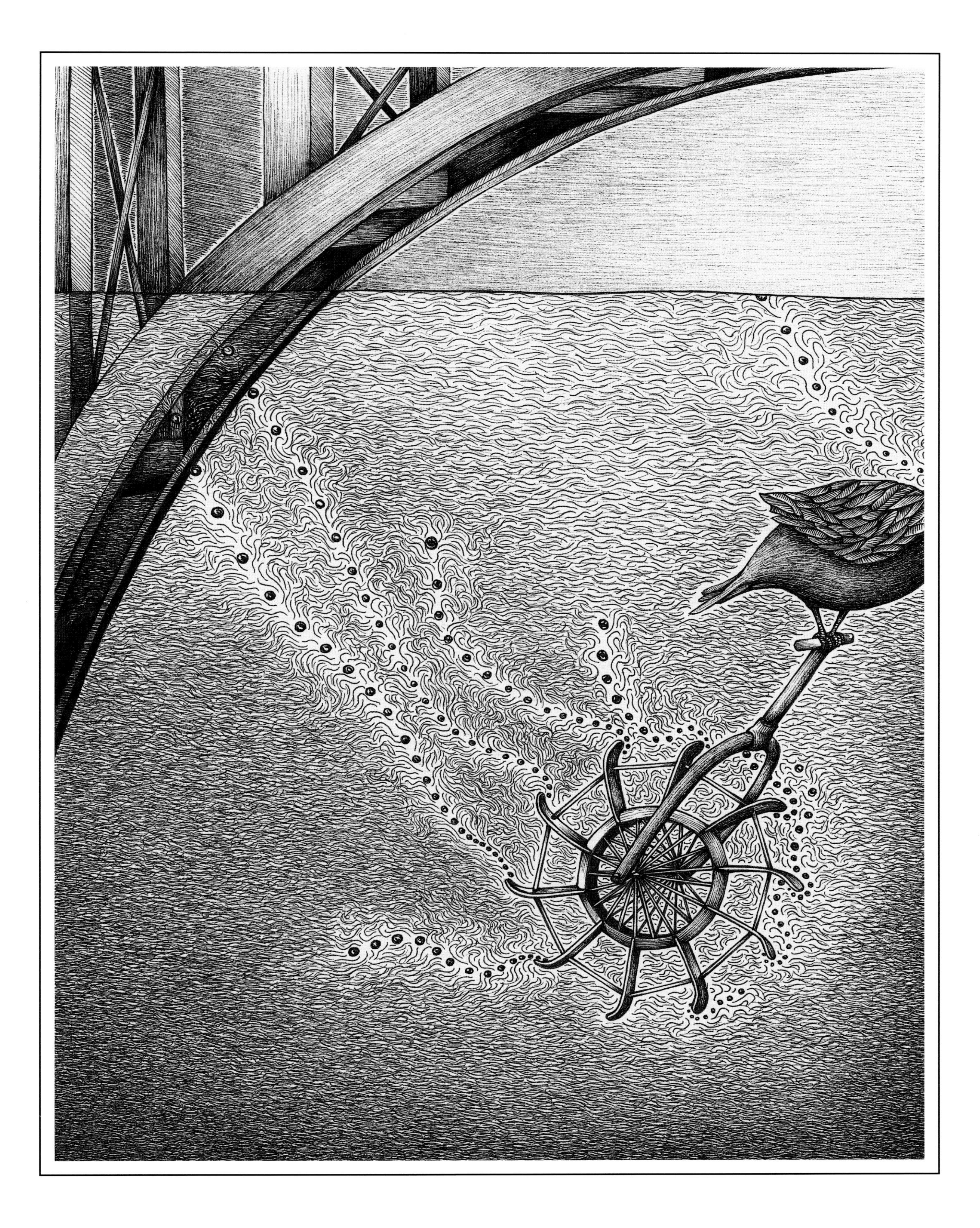

The one they called "Magnificent" had an idea.
Swooshing, he left SEVEN behind.

The one they called "Shows Great Promise" figured it out.

Squeaking, she left SIX behind.

The one they called “Extraordinary” found a solution.
Floating, he left FIVE behind.

The one they called "Outstanding" devised a plan.

Launching, she left FOUR behind.

The one they called "Highly Satisfactory" had little trouble.
Drifting, he left THREE behind.

The one they called "Exceptional" thought it was simple.
Swinging, she left TWO behind.

The one they called "Remarkable" came up with a design.
Flapping, he left ONE behind.

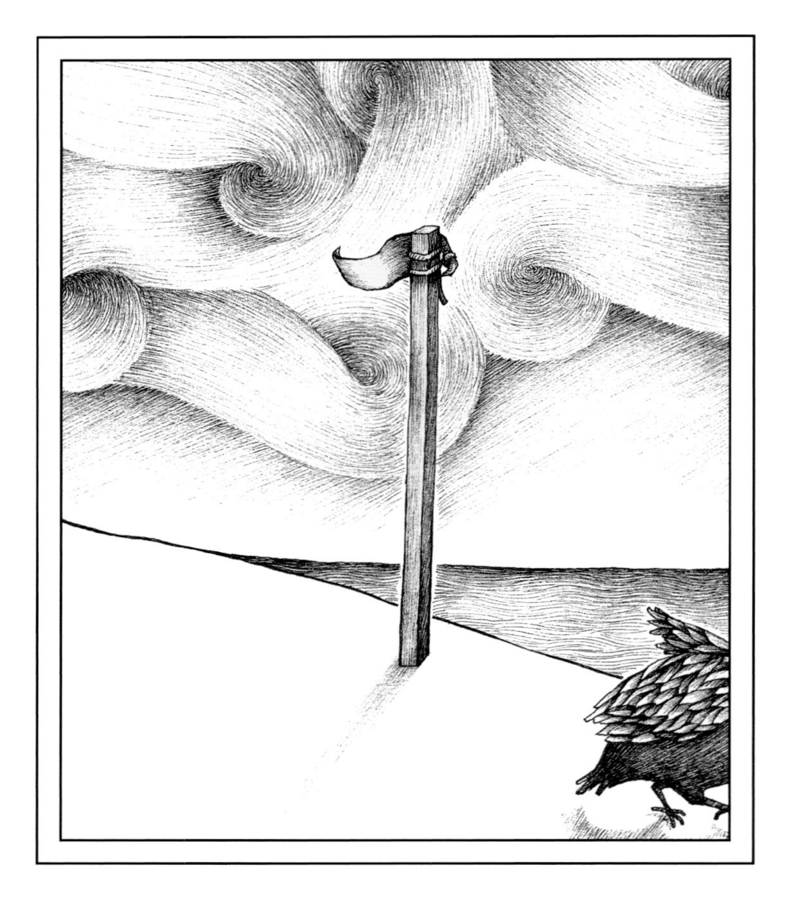

And the one they called "Needs Improvement"
got to the other side just the same ...
leaving none behind.

10 9 8 7 6 5 4 3